W9-AJT-265

Vinge, Joan D. Copy 2

I
VI

Star wars: return of
the Jedi

DATE		
		SEP 26 1984
JUL 20 1983	MAY 07 1984	OCT. 27 1984
JUL 23 1983	MAY 09 1984	JY 22 '88
AUG 31 1983	MAY 23 1984	FE 25 '89
OCT. 15 1983	JUN 06 1984	JUL 25 '94
NOV. 17 1983		
DEC. 21 1983	JUN 23 1984	FEB 22 '95
JAN. 6 1984	JUL 11 1984	SEP 04 '06
JAN. 20 1984	JUL 20 1984	SEP 18 '06
JAN. 25 1984	AUG 9 1984	NO 26 '07
FEB 08 1984	AUG 23 1984	JY 21 '07
FEB. 29 1984	SP. 14 1984	MR 08 '08
MAR. 14 1984		MI 05 '09

EAU CLAIRE DISTRICT LIBRARY

© THE BAKER & TAYLOR CO.

STAR WARS
RETURN OF THE JEDI
™

THE STORYBOOK
BASED ON THE MOVIE

Random House ⌂ New York

88111

EAU CLAIRE DISTRICT LIBRARY 3460 12

7/6/83 B+T 7⁹⁹

Based on the film *Return of the Jedi*
Screenplay by Lawrence Kasdan and George Lucas
Story by George Lucas

Storybook adaptation by Joan D. Vinge

Copyright © 1983 Lucasfilm Ltd. (LFL). All rights reserved under International and Pan-American Copyright Conventions. Published in the United States by Random House, Inc., New York, and simultaneously in Canada by Random House of Canada Limited, Toronto.

Library of Congress Cataloging in Publication Data: Vinge, Joan D. The return of the Jedi. Sequel to: The Empire strikes back storybook. SUMMARY: In a sequel to "The Star Wars Storybook" and "The Empire Strikes Back Storybook," Luke Skywalker and his friends in the Rebel Alliance formulate a daring plan to battle with the Empire and its evil leaders, Darth Vader and the Emperor.
[1. Science fiction] I. Return of the Jedi (Motion picture) II. Title.
PZ7.V7457Re 1983   [Fic]   82–20538
ISBN: 0–394–85624–4 (trade); 0–394–95624–9 (lib. bdg.)
Manufactured in the United States of America
TM—Trademarks of LFL used by Random House, Inc., under authorization.   2 3 4 5 6 7 8 9 0

Han Solo
Captain of the *Millennium Falcon* and a former smuggler; now a general in the Rebel Alliance

Luke Skywalker
A Rebel pilot and the last Jedi Knight

Princess Leia Organa
A leader in the Rebellion against the Galactic Empire

Wicket
An Ewok, a native of the moon Endor

Lando Calrissian
The former Administrator of Cloud City, now a Rebel general

Jabba the Hutt
The intergalactic gangster who rules Tatooine

Artoo-Detoo (R2-D2)
A computer-repair droid who speaks only in electronic sounds
See-Threepio (C-3PO)
An interpreter-droid who speaks six million languages

Darth Vader
The evil Imperial Lord, master of the dark side of the Force

Chewbacca
A two-hundred-year-old Wookiee and co-pilot of the *Millennium Falcon*

Yoda
The Jedi Master who taught Luke the ways of the Force

Long ago, in a galaxy far, far away, the leaders of the Rebel Alliance were gathering to plan the next move in their battle against the evil Galactic Empire. The Rebels had been fighting the Empire and its cruel leader for a long time. They were trying to win freedom for all the worlds the Empire oppressed, but they were badly outnumbered.

Led by Luke Skywalker, a heroic pilot, they had destroyed the Empire's biggest weapon, an armored battle station called the Death Star. The Death Star could destroy whole planets. But since that victory, things had not gone well for the Rebels. The Imperial fleet had driven them out of one hiding place after another. Now the Rebels hoped to join forces for another major victory. They desperately needed one to keep the Rebellion alive.

The Rebels did not know that, even as they met in secret, the Emperor was planning their doom. He had ordered his forces to build a new Death Star. It would be even more powerful than the first one. Once it was operational, his Imperial forces would crush the Rebellion once and for all. . . .

An Imperial Star Destroyer moved toward the monstrous superstructure of the half-finished Death Star. Darth Vader, the Dark Lord of the Sith, was on board the destroyer. He had come to check on the progress of construction at the battle station. He boarded a shuttle and flew toward the waiting Death Star.

The Death Star commander, Moff Jerjerrod, was a tall, confident officer. But the sight of Darth Vader coming on board his battle station was enough to make even Jerjerrod turn pale and tremble. Vader was huge, and his face was hidden behind a mask. He was dressed all in black, and the sound of his harsh mechanical breathing echoed loudly in the silence of the hall.

Darth Vader had a reputation as terrifying as his physical appearance. He controlled the dark side of the Force better than anyone except the Emperor. He could use the Force to kill a man just by looking at him. He could make his subjects do anything he wanted them to, just by willing it. No one could resist him.

Jerjerrod knew that Vader had come to make sure the Death Star was finished on time. And people who failed the Dark Lord did not live to tell about it. "Lord Vader," he said, "my men can't work any faster. The Emperor asks for the impossible."

Vader's faceless mask hissed, "Perhaps you could explain that to him when he arrives."

Jerjerrod gasped. "The Emperor is coming here?"

Vader nodded. "And he will be quite unhappy if you are still behind schedule when he arrives."

"We shall double our efforts!"

"I hope so, Commander," Vader said, "for your sake. The Emperor wants no more delays in the final destruction of the Outlaw Rebellion."

In another part of the galaxy, the two droids Artoo-Detoo and See-Threepio were walking forlornly along a desolate road on the desert planet of Tatooine. The droids had been sent to the court of the arch-criminal Jabba the Hutt by Luke Skywalker. Jabba held Luke's friend Han Solo prisoner. The Rebel Lando Calrissian had tried to rescue Han already, but he had never returned.

The two droids knew that fact very well as they came to the massive gate of Jabba's palace and knocked.

"Why couldn't Chewbacca have delivered this message?" Threepio complained. "No one worries about what happens to droids! Sometimes I wonder why we put up with it all."

Jabba's lieutenant, Bib Fortuna, met the droids and took them to the throne room. The collection of courtiers who stood watching them there was truly terrifying. The worst sight of all was Jabba himself, a wicked, repulsive blob of fat. Jabba laughed evilly when he saw the frightened droids, and called them up before his throne.

With a low whistle, Artoo projected his hologram of Luke. The ten-foot-tall image faced Jabba and said, "I am Luke Skywalker, Jedi Knight and friend of Captain Solo. I wish to meet with Your Greatness to bargain for his life. As a token of my goodwill, I give these two droids to you as a gift." His image disappeared.

"Oh, no!" Threepio cried. "This can't be!" He couldn't believe that Luke would be so cruel.

But Jabba only laughed again. "There will be no bargain," he said. "I don't

plan to give up my favorite decoration." He looked toward an alcove on the wall. There hung Han Solo, still inside the coffinlike carbon-freezing unit where Darth Vader had imprisoned him. "But I will find uses for these droids."

See-Threepio was a translator droid. Jabba knew that he had been programed to speak six million different languages. So Jabba forced Threepio to stand by his throne and act as a translator. Threepio did not like being separated from his companion, Artoo, who had been taken away to serve on Jabba's Sail Barge.

How could things get any worse? Threepio thought to himself. But then the miserable droid saw something that answered his question. Bib came into the hall with a strange bounty hunter— and the bounty hunter's captive was Chewbacca the Wookiee, Han Solo's co-pilot.

"Greetings, Majestic One," the bounty hunter said. "I am Boushh, and I want fifty thousand for bringing you the Wookiee."

Jabba roared with laughter and spoke in his own language.

"He says twenty-five is all he'll pay . . ." Threepio translated nervously, ". . . plus your life."

Boushh froze. Then, calmly, he reached under his cloak and brought out a small silver ball. The ball hummed strangely. The bounty hunter said, "Tell Jabba he'll have to do better than that, or they'll be picking his smelly hide out of every crack in this room. I'm holding a thermal detonator."

"Oh, dear!" Threepio said. He translated the bounty hunter's words.

Jabba stared at the silver ball. It was beginning to glow with an ominous light. Everyone waited fearfully. At last Jabba grinned. "That bounty hunter is my kind of scum! Tell him thirty-five, no more."

Boushh agreed and turned off the thermal detonator. Everyone was very relieved.

"Join our celebration," Jabba said to him. "I may find other work for you."

Boushh nodded coolly. Boba Fett,

the bounty hunter who had captured Han Solo, glared at him. And Jabba's guards led Chewbacca away to the dungeons.

Late that night a shadowy figure entered Jabba's throne room. Boushh crept past the snoring, drunken courtiers to where the frozen Han Solo hung on the wall. The bounty hunter lowered Han's coffin to the ground. Then, carefully, he moved the decarbonization lever. The hard shell covering Han's face began to melt away. Soon his body was free— but it showed no signs of life as Han

toppled forward onto the floor. Boushh waited tensely for a moment. Then Han's eyes opened suddenly and he began to cough.

"Quiet," Boushh whispered. "Just relax for a moment."

"I can't see!" Han mumbled. "What's happening?" He swayed to his feet.

"You're free of the carbonite and have hibernation sickness." Boushh steadied him with a hand. "Your eyesight will return in time. Come, we must hurry."

Han grabbed the bounty hunter and felt his masked face. "I'm not going

anywhere. Who are you, anyway?"

The bounty hunter took off the helmet. Beneath it was the beautiful face of Princess Leia. She kissed Han tenderly. "Someone who loves you."

"Leia!" Han gasped. "Where are we?"

"Jabba's palace. I've got to get you out of here quick." She took his hand.

"Everything's a blur . . . I'm not going to be much help," Han said.

Leia's heart filled with emotion at the sight of her blinded lover. She loved him partly because of the way he laughed at danger. But to see him like this, so helpless, made her care for him even more. "We'll make it," she said softly.

A sudden noise startled them. Leia stiffened as she turned and saw Jabba with his whole court of monsters, watching them from behind a drawn curtain.

"What is it?" asked Han. But then he heard Jabba laugh. "I know that laugh," he said grimly.

"What a touching sight," sneered Jabba.

Han pulled Leia closer to him. "Listen, Jabba, I was on my way back to pay off my debt to you when I got a little sidetracked. I know we've had our differences, but I'm sure we can work this out. . . ."

"It's too late, Solo. You may have been the best smuggler in the business, but you're Bantha fodder now." Jabba signaled his guards. "Take him. I'll decide how to kill him later."

Han and Leia struggled as the guards surrounded them. "I'll pay you triple!" Han shouted. "Jabba, you're giving up a fortune. Don't be a fool." But the guards led him away.

Another guard came to take Leia away. She betrayed no emotion when she saw his face—it was Lando Calrissian, in disguise.

"Wait!" Jabba called. "Bring her to me."

Leia and Lando stopped. Lando looked worried. "I'll be all right," Leia whispered.

Lando glanced at Jabba. "I'm not so sure," he replied. But there was nothing they could do.

As Han was thrown into his prison cell, he heard a loud growl. He jumped back against the cell door, looking around with useless eyes. Then something grabbed him, lifting him off the ground with a roar of joy.

"Chewie, is that you?" Han said in disbelief. His co-pilot barked happily. "What's going on around here, anyway?" he asked as Chewie set him down. The last thing he remembered was that he and Leia had been captured by Darth Vader, back in Cloud City on Bespin. He had thought that he was as good as dead and that he had lost Leia forever.

The eight-foot-tall Wookiee told him that Lando and Luke had made plans for his rescue.

"Lando and Luke?" First Leia and Chewie, now Lando and Luke, all risking their lives to save him. For a moment Han was speechless. In all his years as a smuggler, the only one he had ever trusted completely was Chewbacca—

because Chewie wasn't human. Han had never really had much faith in any human being except himself. But then, he had never had friends like these, who cared so much about him. Maybe helping the Rebel Alliance hadn't been such a foolish gamble after all. But he'd never admit it. He had a reputation to protect. "Is Luke crazy?" he said. "Why'd you listen to him? That kid can't even take care of himself."

Chewie barked a reply.

"Luke, a Jedi Knight?" Han didn't believe it. He knew Luke was a nice kid and a terrific pilot. But Jedi Knights had mysterious powers that came from the Force. "Come on. I'm out of it for a little while and everybody gets delusions."

Chewie growled, insisting that it was true.

"I'll believe it when I see it." Han grinned feebly. "If you'll excuse the expression."

Luke Skywalker entered Jabba's palace, dressed in the robes of a Jedi Knight. The guards could not stop him, although they tried. Luke merely lifted his hand and the guards began to choke. As he passed he lowered his hand and they began to breathe again. Luke had become a true Jedi. The Jedi Master, Yoda, had taught him how to use the Force. He could make all of Jabba's guards do what he wanted with a wave of his hand—even Bib Fortuna, who tried to block his path.

Luke raised his hand. His blue eyes stared into Bib's. "You will take me to Jabba now!"

"I will take you to Jabba now," Bib droned. He could not resist. He took Luke to Jabba.

Jabba was furious when he saw what Luke had done. "Your powers will not work on me, boy," he warned. And it was true.

But Luke was not worried. He glanced at Leia, chained to Jabba's throne, and she nodded at him. "I am taking Cap-

tain Solo and his friends," Luke said. "I warn you not to doubt my powers."

"There will be no bargain, young Jedi," Jabba snapped. "I shall enjoy watching you die." He pressed a hidden button. The floor dropped out from under Luke, and he fell into a pit.

A Rancor, a hideous beast with knifelike teeth, was waiting in the pit. The crowd of courtiers rushed to the edge of the pit to watch it attack Luke. Luke leaped straight up as the Rancor came toward him, using his Jedi training to catch hold of the pit's overhead grate. But the courtiers smashed at his fingers until he fell down into the pit again. He landed in the monster's eye. It bellowed with pain as Luke dropped to the floor. Luke grabbed a bone as the Rancor caught hold of him and lifted him up to its gaping jaws. Quickly he wedged the bone into the beast's mouth.

Roaring, it threw him down, and Luke ran for a metal door at the side of the pit. The Rancor pulled the bone from its throat and came rushing after him. Luke pulled the door open with super-human strength and saw another gate beyond it, with guards on the other side. Luke was trapped. He picked up a skull from the floor and threw it at the control panel on the wall just as the Rancor came through the doorway behind him. The heavy metal door came crashing down on its head, and the Rancor was dead. Luke was safe—for the moment.

Up in the throne room Jabba seethed with fury. "Get the Jedi out of there!" he ordered his guards. "Bring me Solo and the Wookiee. They will *all* suffer for this outrage!"

Luke, Han, and Chewbacca, surrounded by guards on a tiny skiff, looked

out at the endless sea of sand dunes. They were awaiting the fate that Jabba had decreed for them—to be thrown into the Great Pit of Carkoon. It was the nesting place of a giant creature called a Sarlacc, which would eat them all alive. Jabba's huge Sail Barge floated nearby.

"I think my sight is getting better," Han said, trying to sound cheerful. "Instead of a big dark blur, I see a big bright blur."

"You're not missing anything," Luke answered. "I grew up here." He thought about the innocent farm boy he had once been, longing for adventure. He had even dreamed of running away to join the Rebellion. Then his aunt and uncle had been killed by Imperial stormtroopers, and their farm destroyed. And his father. . . . Luke had never imagined that so much would have

happened to him by the time he returned to Tatooine.

"And now we're going to die out here," Han muttered.

"I wasn't planning on it," Luke said evenly. "I had to get you out of Jabba's palace—it was too well guarded. Just stay close to Chewie and Lando. We'll take care of everything." Lando stood nearby on the skiff, still posing as a guard.

"I can hardly wait." Han didn't sound very eager.

Luke looked back toward the gigantic barge where Jabba rode like a sultan. He searched for a glimpse of Leia. If his plan failed, his friends would suffer along with him—and the Rebellion would lose some of its best leaders. But they had all insisted on helping to save Han. *Friends helping each other,* he thought as the Sarlacc pit came into view. *That's part of what the Force means.*

Leia, Threepio, and Artoo watched from Jabba's floating antigravity barge as the skiff carrying their friends approached the huge sand pit where the Sarlacc lived. At the bottom of the pit they could see its great slimy mouth waiting for the prisoners. As guards pushed Luke out onto a plank above the pit, Jabba and his courtiers rushed to the rail to watch. Unnoticed, Artoo zipped to the edge of the barge.

Luke waved good-bye to his friends. At that signal, Artoo launched Luke's lightsaber—a new one that Luke had made himself and had hidden inside Artoo. In the same instant Luke jumped from the plank. Using his Jedi skills, he caught the plank's end as he fell. It

tossed him high up into the air. He did a complete flip, then landed in the skiff again and caught his lightsaber. He ignited it and attacked the startled guards. Lando joined in the fight as Luke freed Han and Chewie.

Furious, Jabba ordered the barge's guns to fire on the skiff. Leia rose and threw the chain that held her prisoner around Jabba's neck. Before he could stop her, she leaped off the throne, pulling the chain tight. Jabba's huge eyes bulged and his slimy tongue flopped out of his mouth as Leia strangled him. His tail slammed down on the deck one last time—and he was dead. Leia began to try to get free of her chains.

The bounty hunter Boba Fett, who

EAU CLAIRE DISTRICT LIBRARY

was aboard the barge, used his rocket pack to fly to the skiff. He fired a metal cable that wrapped itself around Luke's body, but Luke used his lightsaber to cut himself free. Just then gunfire from the barge hit the skiff, knocking the bounty hunter out and wounding Chewbacca. The skiff rocked in the air, throwing Lando overboard into the Sarlacc pit. Lando shouted for help. Han and Chewbacca struggled to the rail of the skiff to save him while Luke leaped across to Jabba's barge.

The wounded Wookiee barked directions to Han, who found a rifle and picked it up. Just then Boba Fett got to his feet. Blindly, Han tried to shoot him with the rifle. He hit Boba's rocket pack instead. It fired, sending the bounty hunter high up into the air. He crashed into the side of Jabba's barge and fell past Lando into the Sarlacc's waiting mouth.

"I wish I could have seen that," Han said regretfully. A second later another round of gunfire hit the skiff and knocked Han overboard. But his famous luck didn't desert him—his foot caught in the railing. He dangled above Lando in the pit. "Lando!" he shouted. "Grab the rifle!"

Gunfire hit the skiff again, shaking the injured Chewie, who was reaching over the rail for Han, who was reaching for Lando. Every time Lando tried to grab Han's rifle, he slid farther down

into the pit. A tentacle from the Sarlacc caught Lando's leg and began to pull him toward its mouth.

Meanwhile, Luke had pulled himself up the barge's side and climbed aboard. Up on its deck, Artoo had found Leia and cut her chains. As the princess and the droid ran across the barge, they saw Threepio being attacked by one of Jabba's creatures. Artoo fired a charged ray at the bully and sent him running.

The barge gunners had Lando, Han, and Chewie in their sights just as Luke reached the gun. He attacked the gunners with his lightsaber. A guard shot the laser sword out of his hand. Luke looked down and saw that his artificial hand was damaged. But it still worked.

The barge's other gun began to fire at the guards. Leia had captured it and was helping Luke. The young Jedi caught up his lightsaber and finished off the guards. "Leia!" he shouted. "Point your gun down! Destroy the barge!" Hear-

ing his order, Artoo and Threepio jumped overboard into the sand.

Lando had managed to grab the end of Han's rifle and was struggling to hang on. Very carefully, Han aimed his laser pistol at the tentacle wrapped around Lando's leg.

"Wait!" Lando cried as the gun wavered dangerously. "I thought you said you were blind."

"Trust me." Han fired. His eyesight had gotten better and his aim was perfect. Lando was free! His friends pulled him on board just as Luke and Leia swung onto the skiff from the barge. The barge began to explode again and again. Using a magnet, the friends quickly rescued the two droids from the sand, and they all sailed away across the desert.

A sandstorm came up out of nowhere as the skiff neared the place where Luke and the others had hidden their starships. They left the skiff and struggled

on foot through the stinging, wind-blown sand to reach the *Millennium Falcon* and Luke's X-wing fighter. They stood together below the *Falcon*'s gangplank and said their last good-byes as they got ready to go their separate ways again.

"Thanks for coming after me, Luke," Han said quietly. He still could not quite believe that Luke and the others had risked so much just to rescue him.

Luke smiled warmly. "Think nothing of it."

Han shook his head. "No, I'm thinking a lot about it. That carbon freeze was the closest thing to dead there is. Now, coming back . . . well, my eyes aren't all that's seeing different, buddy."

Luke felt the change in Han, and he knew that everything he and the others had risked had been worth it. *"Solo" means "alone,"* he thought. He had often wondered whether that was Han's real name. Maybe it was an alias Han had chosen—one that Han felt described him better than his real name. But now Han knew that he didn't have to be a loner anymore. And Luke knew how important that was. "I'll see you all back at the fleet," Luke said. "Right now I have to keep a promise to an old friend."

Leia hugged him warmly. "Hurry back. The entire Alliance should be assembled by now."

"I will," Luke said. He and Artoo climbed into his X-wing and took off. The rest went on board the *Millennium Falcon.* Han patted his ship as he climbed up the ramp. "You're looking good, old girl. I never thought I'd live to see you again."

The *Millennium Falcon* followed Luke's ship into space.

Far across the galaxy thousands of Imperial troops stood at attention inside the Death Star's docking bay as the Emperor arrived. Even Darth Vader kneeled as the sinister figure passed by him. The Emperor ordered him to rise.

"The Death Star will be ready on schedule, my Master," Vader said.

"You have done well." The Emperor nodded. "Now I sense that you wish to search for young Skywalker. Be patient. In time *he* will seek *you* out . . . and you must bring him to me. Only together can we turn him to the dark side of the Force."

"Yes, my Master."

"Everything is happening as I have foreseen." The Emperor chuckled, looking out over the vast line of his troops.

Artoo waited unhappily by Yoda's cottage in the swamps of Dagobah. Luke was inside, visiting the Jedi Master who had trained him.

Luke felt even unhappier than Artoo as he looked into Yoda's face. Al-

though Yoda seemed cheerful, it was clear to Luke that the ancient Jedi Master had become weaker and more frail.

"That face you make," Yoda said. "Look I so bad to young eyes?"

"No, Master," Luke lied. "Of course not."

Yoda chuckled. "I do, yes, I do! Sick I've become. Yes. Old and weak." He pointed a crooked finger at Luke. "When nine hundred years you reach, look as good you will not." He went to his bed. "Soon I will rest forever. Earned it I have."

"You can't die, Master Yoda," Luke said. He realized how much he had grown to love his cantankerous old teacher. "I won't let you."

"Strong with the Force you are . . . but not that strong!" Yoda lay down.

"But I need your help to finish my training." Luke had left Dagobah before Yoda had wanted him to. His growing Jedi powers had told him that Han and Leia were captives of Darth Vader. Saving them had seemed more important than anything to him—then.

"No more training do you need," Yoda said.

"Then I am a Jedi?" Luke asked, surprised. Yoda had warned him that he had not mastered the Force completely.

Yoda shook his head. "Not yet. Vader . . . Vader you must face again. Then a Jedi you'll be. And face him you will, sooner or later."

Luke was pale and silent for a long moment. Finally he was able to ask, "Master Yoda . . . is Darth Vader my father?"

Yoda smiled a strange, sad smile. Luke held his breath as he waited for Yoda to answer.

At last Yoda said, "Your father he is."

Luke jerked as if he had been cut.

"Told you, did he?" Yoda asked.

Luke nodded. When he had fought Darth Vader to save his friends, the Dark Lord had told him that he was his son. Luke had wanted to believe it was only a trick and a lie.

Yoda closed his eyes. "Unexpected this is, and unfortunate. Now a great weakness you carry. Fear for you, I do." Yoda knew that now Luke would doubt himself every time he thought of his father. Luke knew that his father had given in to evil. If his father could not resist it, how could he?

"Master Yoda, I'm sorry I disobeyed you. I shouldn't have left Dagobah before I was ready."

"I know, but face Vader you must, and sorry will not help." Yoda called him closer. "Luke . . . of the Emperor beware, or suffer your father's fate you will. When I am gone . . . last of the Jedi will you be." He lay back again. "Leave me. Tell you the rest Ben will." Yoda sighed deeply. His body shuddered once, and then he disappeared, to rest forever.

Luke went slowly back to his ship. He sat on a log with his head in his hands. He felt very young and confused. "I can't do it. I can't go on alone," he told Artoo.

The voice of Obi-Wan Kenobi said, "Yoda and I will be with you always."

Luke looked up. Ben's shimmering image was before him. It seemed almost real enough to touch. Once Ben had been Luke's teacher, but Ben Kenobi was no longer flesh and blood. He was a part of the Force now.

"Ben!" Luke cried. "Why didn't you tell me the truth?"

Ben shook his head. "I was going to tell you when you had finished your training. But you rushed off unprepared. We warned you about impatience."

"You told me Darth Vader killed my father," Luke said accusingly.

"Your father, Anakin, was lured to the dark side of the Force and became Darth Vader." Ben's voice was gentle. "When that happened, the good man he used to be was lost forever. What I told you was true . . . in a way."

"In a way!" Luke exclaimed.

"Luke, you're going to find that many of the truths we cling to depend greatly on our point of view." Luke did not answer. Ben watched Luke's angry face for a moment. "I don't blame you for being angry. If I was wrong, it wasn't

the first time. You see, what happened to your father was my fault . . . in a way."

Luke was startled. He waited for Ben to explain.

"When I first met your father," Ben said, "he was a great pilot, and the Force was with him very strongly. I tried to train him in the ways of a Jedi. I thought that I could be as good a teacher as Yoda. I was not. The Emperor lured him to the dark side." He stopped and sighed. "My mistake has had terrible consequences for the galaxy."

"There is still good in him," Luke said. He would not believe that his father could not be saved.

"Once I thought so too," said Ben. "But now he is more machine than man, evil and twisted."

"I can't kill my own father!" Luke's hands made fists. He looked down at the artificial one, suddenly remembering how his father had cut his hand off while trying to kill him. He wanted to love his father. But how could he love someone who wanted him dead?

"Then the Emperor has already beaten you, and darkness will prevail," Ben said sadly. "You were our only hope. Yoda felt we could find another, but it is too late. The other Yoda spoke of is your twin sister."

"Sister!" Luke was astonished. He tried to remember, to understand. Then, "Leia is my sister!" he exclaimed.

"Yes," said Ben. "When you were born, I separated you. Your identities were hidden and you were raised apart, to protect you from the Emperor."

Luke could barely breathe. The knowledge of what he had to do ached inside him. "Then I must kill Lord Vader."

Ben nodded. "You cannot escape your destiny. You will have to face Vader again."

As Luke looked into his eyes, Ben gazed at the young Jedi with compassion.

The Rebel fleet stretched across space as far as the eye could see. Inside its largest ship, the Headquarters Frigate, were all the Rebel commanders. They were making plans with Mon Mothma, the stern, beautiful woman who was the leader of the Alliance.

General Lando Calrissian found Han Solo and Chewbacca at last. They were talking to Leia and the two droids. Lando was going to lead the Rebel fleet when it attacked the Death Star.

"I'm surprised they didn't ask you to do it," Lando told Han.

"Maybe they did," Han said. "But I'm not crazy. You're the respectable one, remember?"

Leia took Han's arm protectively. "Han is staying on the command ship with me. We're both very proud of you, Lando."

Mon Mothma called for silence in the room. "The Empire has made a critical mistake," she announced. "The time for our attack has come." She told the commanders that the Alliance had learned where the half-finished Death Star was, and that it was not well protected. They had also been informed that the Emperor was on the Death Star. If they attacked now, the Rebels could capture or kill the Empire's leader! Ex-

citement rippled through the audience.

Admiral Ackbar stepped forward to Mon Mothma's side. He pointed at the holographic model of the Death Star projected in the air. "Although the Death Star is not finished," he said, "it is protected by an energy shield that is generated from the nearby Moon of Endor. No ship can fly through the shield; no weapon can penetrate it. The shield must be shut down before any attack can succeed. Once the shield is down, our fighters can fly into the superstructure and attempt to hit the Death Star's main reactor, somewhere in here. That will destroy it."

The listening Rebels murmured their concern.

"We have acquired a small Imperial shuttle," continued the Admiral. "Under this guise, a strike team will land on Endor and deactivate the shield generator. The control bunker is guarded, but a small squad should be able to overcome their security forces."

"I wonder who they've found to pull that off?" Leia whispered. The job of shutting down the energy shield would be even more dangerous than attacking the Death Star itself.

"General Solo," called the Admiral, "is your strike team ready?"

Leia looked at Han, stunned and then suddenly very proud. He'd become a different person since his rescue. But she had never expected that he would volunteer for such a dangerous and important mission.

"My Rebel fighting squad is ready," Han said, "but I need a command crew for my shuttle." In less than a minute Chewbacca and Leia had volunteered. They were joined by Luke, who had just returned from Dagobah. Threepio and Artoo made the crew complete. Artoo beeped his excitement to Threepio.

"I don't think 'exciting' is the right word," Threepio said nervously.

Leia hugged Luke, welcoming him back. She felt at once the change that had come over him and asked, "What is it, Luke?"

"Nothing," Luke said. "I'll tell you someday." He looked down, away from her eyes. He could not tell anyone, even Leia, about the painful secret he carried—that Darth Vader was their father.

Later that day Lando went to the frigate's docking bay to wish Han and his crew good luck in their mission. Han told him to take the *Millennium Falcon* for his own mission against the Death Star. "I mean it, take her! She used to be yours—she'll bring you luck. Besides, she's the fastest ship in the whole fleet." Han didn't try to hide how proud he was of that fact.

"Thanks, old buddy." Lando grinned. He knew how much the *Millennium*

Falcon meant to Han and what a good ship it was. Han's offer moved him deeply. "I'll take care of her. She won't get a scratch."

Han smiled at his old friend. Once they had been rivals, but now they were bound together by far stronger ties: They had saved each other's lives, and they fought for the same cause. "I've got your word. Not a scratch—on her or you."

Lando laughed. "Get out of here, you pirate." He turned away quickly before Han could see the emotion on his face.

"See ya soon, pal." Han waved and went up the ramp into the stolen Imperial shuttle that would take them all to Endor. He seated himself next to his Wookiee co-pilot. "Okay, Chewie," he said. "Let's find out what this baby can do."

They fired up the engines. The Imperial shuttle moved out of the docking bay into space. It lowered its wings and took off into the night.

Han and his crew came out of hyperspace in a blur of light. Below them they could see the Death Star. Beyond it, floating in space, was the green Moon of Endor. As they flew toward the moon the Imperial forces let them pass through the deflector shield without any questions. "What did I tell you?" Han said. "No sweat." Their disguise worked— or so they thought. They didn't know Darth Vader himself had allowed their ship to land on Endor because he knew that Luke was on board. Luke would finally come to him, as the Emperor had promised. The Emperor controlled the dark side of the Force better than anyone alive. He could foresee everything about the Rebels' plans, and he had prepared a deadly trap for them.

The stolen Imperial shuttle landed in a forest clearing among Endor's giant trees. A hush fell over the Rebels as they left the ship and stood looking up at the trees. The trees were so tall that their tops were lost in the darkness, and so ancient that they made mere human beings feel insignificant. Only Threepio was not moved by their beauty. "No, I *don't* think it's pretty here," he told

Artoo. "With our luck, it's full of droid-eating monsters."

Han led the Rebel squad toward the bunker where the shield generator lay. But then they spotted Imperial scouts with speeder bikes blocking their way.

Without waiting to talk it over, Han attacked the scouts. The others were forced to join in the fight to rescue him. Luke and Leia jumped on a speeder bike and took off after two of the Imperial scouts who had escaped. If the scouts warned the bunker, the Rebels' plans would be ruined.

After a short chase through the trees, Luke and Leia caught up with one Imperial scout. Luke threw the scout off the speeder bike and took control of it. On separate bikes, he and Leia flew on after the remaining scout. But suddenly two more scouts attacked them from a hiding place in the trees.

"Keep on that one!" Luke shouted to Leia. "I'll take these two!"

Luke slammed his speeder bike's steering vanes into the braking mode. The two scouts, caught off guard, flew past him. Luke blasted one scout with his bike's laser cannon. The second scout sped on ahead. Luke followed him grimly.

Meanwhile, Leia flew on between the trees at high speed and caught the other scout. He fired his handgun at her bike and hit it. Leia leaped off as the bike exploded. Intent on watching her fall, the scout flew into a tree and his own bike exploded.

Luke caught up to the last scout. The scout slammed his own bike into Luke's and the two bikes locked together. Suddenly a huge tree trunk loomed ahead of them and Luke could not avoid it. He leaped to safety as the two bikes came apart and his bike hit the tree.

The scout circled back, firing his cannon at Luke. Luke ignited his lightsaber and deflected the bolts with it. As the scout bore down on him he ducked aside at the last moment. He chopped off the bike's steering vane with his saber, and the last scout crashed.

When Luke finally found his way back to Han and the Rebel squad, he was upset to learn that Leia had not returned. He began a search for her with Han, Chewie, and the droids.

But Leia had already been found. As she slowly awakened after her fall, she saw a fuzzy little alien face with big brown eyes peering into her own. Leia sat up, groaning. The tiny creature leaped back, holding up his spear. His name was Wicket, and he was an Ewok. The Ewoks lived on Endor. They were afraid of humans because the Imperial troops had killed many of their tribe.

"Hey, I won't hurt you," Leia called.

She shook her head to clear it and got to her feet. She ached all over. "I think I got off at a good time," she said, circling the twisted wreckage of her bike. "You don't happen to have a comlink, do you?" she asked Wicket with a rueful smile.

The creature followed her like a puppy, seeming more curious than afraid now.

Just then she heard a twig snap in the underbrush and pulled out her gun. Wicket hid under a log as Leia turned and saw an Imperial scout step into the clearing, his gun pointed at her. The scout took away Leia's gun, and suddenly Wicket leaped out from the log and stabbed the scout in the leg. In the confusion, Leia managed to knock her captor down and shoot him.

Wicket looked up at her in awe. He took Leia's hand and led her away into the trees toward his village.

A short time later Han and the others found the forest clearing where Leia had crashed. There was no trace of her now. But Chewbacca picked up a scent with his sensitive nose and led them on into the forest.

He did not lead them to Leia, but to several pieces of meat hanging from a pole.

"Great, Chewie!" grumbled Han. "Always thinking of your stomach!" He was far more worried than he would admit about Leia's disappearance.

As the Wookiee reached for a piece of meat Luke shouted, "No, wait!"

But it was too late. Chewie had set off a trap. Before they knew it, they were hanging high in the air in an Ewok net. Artoo quickly cut through the net, and they all fell to the ground. When they caught their breath, they found that they were surrounded by Ewoks with spears. The Ewoks took away their guns. Wicket, who was with the other Ewoks, said nothing. He wasn't sure if these were Leia's friends, or the Ewoks' enemies.

But when the Ewoks saw Threepio, they began to gasp and chatter to one another. Threepio, who knew millions of languages, spoke to them in their own little-known dialect. When they heard him, the Ewoks dropped their spears and lay down on the ground before him. Then they began to chant to him.

"What did you say to them?" Han asked, amazed.

Threepio looked startled. "I could be mistaken . . . but I believe they think I'm some sort of god."

"Well, if they think you're a god, tell them to let us go," Han said impatiently.

"That wouldn't be proper, Captain Solo," Threepio answered. "It's against my programing to pretend I'm a god."

Han started toward Threepio threateningly, but the Ewoks leaped forward

and stopped him with their spears. They tied everyone but Threepio to long poles and carried them to their village. They made a litter for Threepio and carried him like a king.

When they reached their village deep in the forest, the Ewoks tried to decide what to do with their captives. Chirpa, the Ewok chief, and Logray, the med-icine man, wanted to roast Han for dinner. Leia, who had come to the village with Wicket, tried to change their minds, but they refused to listen.

"Luke, what can we do?" Leia asked desperately.

"Threepio," Luke said, "tell them to let us go or you'll get angry and use your magic."

"What magic, Master Luke?" the droid asked nervously. "I couldn't—"

"Tell them!" Luke ordered.

Threepio repeated Luke's words. The Ewoks chattered and shook their heads in disbelief. Then the litter on which Threepio sat rose into the air and began to spin. "Help! Artoo, help me!" he called.

The frightened Ewoks let the prisoners go, and Leia ran to them. Still using the Force to control the litter, Luke lowered poor Threepio to the ground. "Thanks, Threepio," he said with a smile.

Shaken, the golden droid exclaimed, "Why . . . why . . . I had no idea I had it in me."

That evening the Ewoks gathered in their firelit meeting-lodge to hear Luke and his friends explain their mission on Endor. Threepio told the tiny creatures about the terrible things the Empire had done, and about the Rebel Alliance that was fighting the Empire. When he finished speaking, Wicket made a speech of his own, urging his people to help the Rebels. Chief Chirpa and the Ewok elders nodded their agreement. They would be glad to have the cruel Imperial troops gone from their world. With a pounding of drums and much cheering, the Ewoks made the Rebels honorary members of their tribe. And they promised to show them the quickest way to the shield generator.

Luke quietly left the celebration. Leia saw him go and followed him outside.

"What's wrong?" she asked. She knew that something had been troubling him ever since he had come back from Dagobah. As she gazed into his shadowed eyes, she realized how dear he was to her—dearer than she wanted to admit. She loved Han, because Han was all the things that she had never been allowed to be, wild and reckless things. But she couldn't help loving Luke, too, because Luke was so very much like her.

Luke glanced down at the hand she held. It was his artificial one. "Leia, do you remember your mother?"

Surprised, she said, "Yes. Just a little bit. She died when I was very young."

"What do you remember?"

"Just feelings, really . . . images." Leia shook her head.

"Tell me."

"She was very beautiful. Gentle and kind . . . but sad." Remembering her mother's smile and touch made Leia's heart ache. She had lost her mother—and then the Empire had killed her father and all of her family and friends. Darth Vader and the Death Star had blown up her entire world. She would never, never be able to forget it. "Why are you asking me this?" she asked.

Luke let go of her hand and turned away. "I have no memory of my mother. I never knew her."

The sadness in his voice pulled her mind back into the present. "Luke," she said, "tell me what's troubling you."

He took a deep breath. "Vader is here on this moon," he said.

Leia's hands tightened at her sides. "How do you know?" she whispered.

"I can feel it. He's come for me. He feels it when I'm near too." Luke looked at her worried face. "I must leave you, or the whole mission will be in danger." He gazed past her, into the darkness. "I have to face Vader."

"I don't understand," Leia said. "Why?"

Luke moved closer to her. He said gently and calmly, "I want you to know this, because . . . I might not come back.

And you're the only one I can trust. Darth Vader is my father."

"Your father?" Leia felt herself grow pale. She pulled away from him. "No, I can't believe that!" It couldn't be true. Luke was a brave, honorable Jedi Knight. He could not be the son of the inhuman monster who had destroyed her world. She shook her head. "Don't talk that way. You must survive. I do what I can, but I'm of no importance compared to you. You have a special power—I've seen it. The Rebellion needs you."

"No, Leia," Luke said wearily. "The life force runs through all living things. The Rebellion will go on long after I'm gone." His face was full of sorrow. Suddenly he looked much older.

"There's something else you have to

know," said Luke. "The Force is strong in you, Leia, because you are my sister, my twin sister. If I don't return, then you are the last hope for the Alliance."

Leia stood very still, remembering her real mother and her adopted parents. She knew Luke's words were true.

"I must try to save him," Luke said softly. "I'm the only one who can."

Leia closed her eyes. When she opened them again, they were full of tears. "No, Luke, no! It's too dangerous. Run away, far away! I wish I could go with you—" She was startled by her words, but at that moment she believed them.

Luke shook his head. "No, you don't. You've never faltered. You've always been stronger than any of us. You would never run away. And I can't either now. He's my father. There *is* good in him. I have felt it. He won't turn me over to the Emperor. I must try to save him." They held each other close for a moment. "Good-bye, sweet, sweet Leia," he whispered. And then he disappeared into the moonlit forest.

It wasn't long before Luke ran into a squad of Imperial soldiers. He surrendered to them without a fight, knowing they would take him to Darth Vader.

Darth Vader stood waiting on the deck of the Imperial landing platform. His

troops brought Luke to him and then left them alone together.

"The Emperor is expecting you," the Dark Lord said. "He believes you will turn to the dark side."

"I know . . . Father." Luke searched for some glimpse of a face behind Vader's mask. His heart was beating very fast.

"So you have finally accepted the truth."

Luke nodded. "I have accepted the truth that you were once Anakin Skywalker, my father."

"That name no longer has any meaning for me," Vader said.

"It is the name of your true self!" Luke insisted. "You have only forgotten. I know there is good in you. That is why you couldn't kill me. That is why you won't take me to the Emperor now. Come away with me, Father." He moved closer to Vader. *You must have good in you,* he thought, *or how can I?*

Vader ignited Luke's lightsaber and held it between them. He shook his head. His breath hissed loudly in the silence. At last he said, "You do not know the power of the dark side. I must obey my master." Vader knew that if it was necessary, the Emperor would sacrifice him without pity to turn his son to the dark side. But his life, his very soul, were no longer his own.

"I will not join you," Luke said. "You will have to kill me."

"If that is your destiny," Vader answered tonelessly.

"Search your feelings, Father!" Luke cried. "I feel the conflict within you. Let go of your hate."

Vader extinguished the lightsaber and signaled for the guards. "It is too late for me, my son."

Luke bowed his head. He wondered whether the conflict he had felt was only within his own heart. "Then my father is truly dead."

Darth Vader took him away to meet the Emperor.

The next morning Han's Rebel strike squad and the Ewoks gathered on a ridge overlooking the Imperial shield generator. The huge bunker that protected it was all they could see. Four Imperial scouts guarded the bunker's doorway. The Rebels tried to think of a way to get past the guards.

"There're only four guards," Han said. "This should be easy."

"It only takes one to sound the alarm," Leia reminded him. She was remembering his impulsive attack of the day before.

Han grinned. "Then we'll have to get rid of them real quiet-like."

Leia looked at her watch. "We're running out of time. The whole Rebel fleet is in hyperspace by now."

Just then Threepio called, "Oh, Mistress Leia! I'm afraid Paploo has done something rash!"

They looked down the hill just in time to see Paploo, an Ewok scout, run out of the trees and steal one of the guards' speeder bikes. Three of the guards jumped on their own bikes and chased him. Only one was left behind.

Han, Leia, and Chewbacca were amazed and delighted. "Not bad for a little ball of fuzz," Han said admiringly.

Paploo led the guards farther away from the bunker. Deep in the forest he jumped from his speeder bike and escaped. The guards went on chasing the bike through the trees.

Meanwhile, Han and Chewie captured the last guard easily. Leia joined them, and they peered in through the dark entrance to the bunker. It seemed to be empty. They went inside.

On the Death Star, Luke and Darth Vader entered the Emperor's throne room.

"Welcome, young Skywalker," the Emperor said. "I've been expecting you. Soon you will call *me* Master, as your father does."

Luke stared defiantly at the shrunken, grotesque being who had corrupted his father. "You won't make me join the dark side. Soon I will die, and so will you."

The Emperor laughed. "Do you mean because the Rebel fleet will attack us? We are quite safe from them here."

Luke was stunned. How did the Emperor know about the attack? But he only said, "You are too confident. That makes you weak."

"Your faith in your friends on Endor

is *your* weakness," the Emperor said. "They are walking into a trap. And so is the Rebel fleet. Your friends will never destroy the shield generator. An entire legion of my troops is waiting for them." He pointed out the wide window at the moon.

Luke couldn't hide his fear this time as he thought of his friends. He looked at his lightsaber, which Darth Vader had given to the Emperor.

"Everything is happening just as I planned." The Emperor smiled. "The deflector shield will still be operating when the Rebel fleet arrives. And that is only the beginning of my surprise. . . . From here you will watch the final destruction of the Alliance and the end of your pitiful Rebellion." He held the laser sword out to Luke. "You want this, don't you? Go ahead—take your Jedi weapon and kill me. Give in to your anger. The more hatred you feel, the closer you come to joining the dark side."

Luke's hands opened and closed helplessly as he tried to decide what to do. He must kill the Emperor, or his friends and the Rebellion would be lost. But if striking the Emperor down meant turning to the dark side. . . . "No, never," he said. He would not surrender like his father had—he would not!

"You must. It is your destiny." The

Emperor held out the lightsaber. "You, like your father, are now . . . mine."

Luke, Vader, and the Emperor watched from the Death Star as the entire Rebel fleet appeared out of hyperspace.

On board the *Millennium Falcon,* Lando was surprised and worried when his instruments showed him that the deflector shield was still operating. "Pull up!" he ordered his fighter squadrons. "Break off the attack!" They could not reach the Death Star unless the shield was gone. The fighters veered off desperately, barely avoiding a collision with the invisible wall of energy.

At the same time, on board the Rebel Star Cruiser, Admiral Ackbar had discovered an even worse problem. The whole Imperial fleet was waiting for the Rebel forces. Thousands of enemy ships were appearing behind them. The Rebels had fallen into the jaws of a deadly trap. They were caught between the de-flector shield and the Imperial fleet. Unless Han and his squad could destroy the shield generator, they were all doomed.

Meanwhile, Han, Leia, and the Rebels were working to do just that. They had reached the main control room of the shield generator and captured everyone there. They began to set explosives around the room to blow up the generator.

Leia looked up at a screen above the control panel. "Hurry, Han," she called. "The fleet is being attacked!"

Han looked up at the screen. "Blast it! With the shield up, the Empire's got them backed against a wall."

"That is right, Rebel scum," a voice said.

They spun around. Dozens of heavily armed Imperial troops surrounded them.

The Emperor, Darth Vader, and Luke watched the battle rage out in space.

"As you can see, my young apprentice," the Emperor said, "your friends have failed. Now watch the fire power of this fully armed battle station." He put Luke's lightsaber nearby, where Luke could reach it easily.

Luke turned, numb with horror. The Rebels had been tricked! The Death Star's weapons were fully operational, even though the station was only half completed. And now the Emperor was about to use its terrible power against the helpless Rebel fleet! Luke looked back out the window just in time to see a deadly beam of energy shoot out from the Death Star. The beam destroyed a Rebel Star Cruiser as if it were a mere fly.

The *Millennium Falcon* roared by the deflector shield, followed by enemy TIE fighters. Lando watched in disbelief as the Death Star destroyed the Star Cruiser. The shock wave from the explosion rocked his ship. "That thing's operational!" he said into his radio.

"We saw it," Admiral Ackbar's voice answered grimly. "All craft get ready to retreat. We can't face the Death Star."

"Han will get the shield down, Admiral," Lando said. "We can't give up and run yet! We've got to give him more

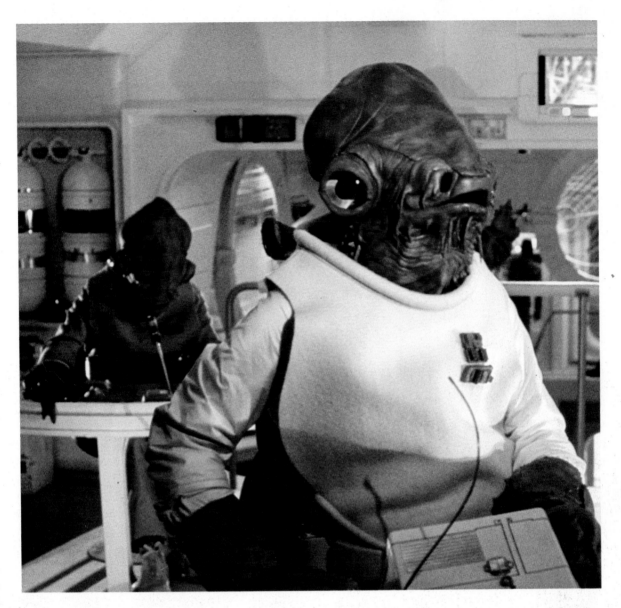

time. Order our ships to move closer to the Imperial fleet. Then the Death Star can't fire at us without hitting their own ships."

"All right," said Admiral Ackbar. "We're going to stay and fight."

The Emperor's high, piercing laughter was the only sound in the Death Star's throne room. "Your fleet is lost," he said to Luke, "and your friends will all die. If they do manage to blow up the shield generator, I have ordered this battle station to destroy Endor."

Luke's eyes were full of rage. His lightsaber began to shake where it lay as he fought his own battle with the dark side of himself.

The Emperor smiled. "Good," he whispered. "Strike me down with your hatred, and join the dark side."

Luke could stop himself no longer. The lightsaber flew into his hand. But as he struck at the Emperor, Darth Vader's laser sword blocked his blow. Luke turned to fight his father at last.

As Han, Leia, and Chewbacca were led from the bunker by the Imperial troops, Wicket and hundreds of Ewoks

attacked the Imperial forces. The Ewoks were tiny and weak compared to the armored Imperial troops. They had only spears and other primitive weapons to use against the Imperial blasters and gigantic two-legged AT-ST walkers. But the tiny natives knew every inch of their forest world and how to use it against their enemies. They tangled the stormtroopers in vines. They led them into pits and traps. They crushed their equipment under falling logs. Soon the Imperial troops were fighting for their lives.

In the midst of the battle that followed, Han, Leia, and Chewie managed to escape from their Imperial

guards. Han and Leia rushed to the bunker door terminal. They would need Artoo to work it so that the door would open. Han signaled to Artoo and Threepio and they came rushing over. But just as they got to the door, Artoo was hit by an explosion. As Threepio tried to help his wounded friend, Han rushed over to the control terminal. "Maybe I can hotwire this thing," he said desperately.

In the throne room Luke and his father fought their own desperate battle as the

Emperor watched. Luke's powers were as strong as his father's now, and just as deadly. At last Luke's father stumbled and dropped his lightsaber. Luke stood above him, ready to attack.

"Go on!" the Emperor hissed. "Let the hate flow through you."

Luke looked up at the Emperor, suddenly realizing that he was doing just what the evil ruler wanted him to do. The Emperor wanted him to kill his own father. That was the unforgivable act that would make him belong to the dark side forever. Luke lowered his sword.

Vader attacked Luke again, forcing Luke to defend himself. Luke took cover behind the Emperor's throne. "I will not fight you, Father. Take my weapon." He threw his lightsaber onto the floor.

"I do not believe you will destroy me."

Vader picked up the weapon. "Give yourself to the dark side, Luke," he said. "It is the only way you can save your friends. I know your thoughts. Your feelings for them are strong, especially for . . . Leia! You love her. Obi-Wan was wise to hide her. If you will not turn to the dark side, perhaps she will." He knew his son's emotions. He knew exactly how to stir Luke's anger and fear.

"Never!" Luke cried. His lightsaber flew back to him, and he attacked his father harder than before. Sparks flew and the air crackled with energy. He struck the lightsaber from Vader's grasp and it flew into the deep shaft at the center of the room. Luke saw his father's useless, broken mechanical hand.

He looked down at his own artificial hand. *I'm becoming just like him,* he thought. He held his lightsaber at his father's throat.

"Kill him!" cried the Emperor. "Take your father's place at my side."

Luke looked at the Emperor and back at his father. Then he made the choice that he had been preparing for all his life. He hurled his saber away. "No," he said. "I will never turn to the dark side. You have failed, Your Highness. I am a Jedi, as my father was before me."

The Emperor's face twisted with rage. "Then if you will not be turned," he said, "you will be destroyed!" Blinding bolts of energy shot from his hands and struck Luke down.

Darth Vader crawled, like a wounded animal, to the Emperor's side.

"Hold it! Don't move." Five Imperial troopers appeared at the bunker entrance where Han and Leia were still working feverishly at the control panel. The two Rebels froze when they saw that they were surrounded. Outside the Ewoks were still fighting the enemy forces, but for the two Rebels the battle was over—and they had lost it.

"You know I love you," Han said, wishing he had said it a thousand times before this moment. Leia nodded, her eyes filled with understanding and love. And then they both spun around, drawing their laser guns, and fired together.

Somehow, miraculously, they managed to shoot all five troopers, but one of the enemy wounded Leia. Han rushed to her side when he heard her cry out. Then a new sound made him look up. He saw a giant Imperial walker standing over them, aiming its guns. He shielded Leia uselessly with his body. But then the walker's hatch opened and Chewbacca stuck his head out.

Han had never been happier to see his co-pilot. "All right!" he shouted. "Let's get that shield down!"

Luke lay still under the Emperor's blinding energy bolts. The ruler of the dark side smiled in triumph. He was

sure that the young Jedi was dead at last. "Young fool!" he hissed. "You were no match for the power of the dark side. You have paid the price for failing to see that." He moved to stand over Luke's body.

But suddenly Vader leaped to his feet and grabbed the Emperor from behind. The Emperor struck out at him wildly. Energy bolts shot from his hands, but they went out of control. The white lightning struck Darth Vader, flowing down over his black cape like rain.

Calling up all of his strength, Vader carried the Emperor to the pit at the center of the room and threw him into it. Far down in the pit the Emperor's body exploded.

Wounded by the terrible blasts of energy, Darth Vader swayed in the rush of wind at the edge of the pit. Luke pulled his father away to safety. Then father and son lay side by side, too weak to move.

Out in space Lando saw the image of the deflector shield disappear from his computer's screen. "The shield is down! Red Group, Gold Group, follow me. We're going to attack the Death Star's main reactor." He grinned at his co-

pilot. "I told you they'd do it!"

Lando and the Rebel fleet swarmed toward the Death Star. Their weapons blasted the unprotected battle station, causing explosion after explosion.

Inside the station Imperial troops ran frantically in all directions, looking for some way to escape. The hallways shook and rumbled. Flames leaped up on every side. Luke struggled to carry his father's huge, weakening body through the chaos toward an Imperial shuttle. Finally he collapsed. He could go no farther.

"Go on, my son," his father whispered. "Leave me."

"No," Luke said. "I've got to save you!"

"You already have, Luke."

Luke shook his head. "Father, I won't leave you." His voice trembled. The sound of explosions was getting nearer.

Darth Vader pulled him close. "Luke, help me take this mask off."

"You'll die," Luke protested.

"Nothing can stop that now. Just once, let me face you without it. Let me look on you with my own eyes."

Slowly Luke took off his father's mask. Beneath it he saw the face of a sad old man, whose eyes were full of love.

"It's too late, Luke, too late!" his father gasped. "I want to die. I could not bear to live on like this in your world. . . . Save yourself!" And Darth Vader, Anakin Skywalker . . . Luke's father, died.

A huge explosion shook the Death Star. Luke rose shakily to his feet and stumbled toward a shuttle.

The *Millennium Falcon* flew at top speed over the endless surface of the Death Star. Lando and his backup fighters fought their way toward the one spot where he could fire a missile and hit the battle station's main reactor. That was the only way to destroy the Death Star. The fighters held the enemy at bay while Lando drew closer and closer, until at last he was on target. He fired his missiles. "Direct hit!" he shouted triumphantly. The *Millennium Falcon* shot up and away from the Death Star. Now Lando had only seconds to escape

before the battle station exploded. But the *Millennium Falcon* was a fast ship—seconds were all he needed.

Just ahead of him, as he flew toward the Rebel fleet, was an Imperial shuttle—with Luke Skywalker on board.

On Endor, Han, Leia, and their friends saw the flash as the Death Star exploded out in space. They knew then that the Rebels had won.

Late that night there was a big party in the Ewok village. Everyone danced and laughed and sang, celebrating the Rebel victory.

Han, Leia, and Chewbacca waited at the edge of the firelit village square for Luke and Lando. Lando and two Rebel pilots came down the forest path at last,

and from another direction Luke arrived. Their friends ran to greet them. So did Threepio and Artoo. They all stood close together, weary but joyful. They had traveled a long, hard road together, but it had led them to victory.

Only Luke did not seem to feel the happiness the others shared. He gazed silently into the forest, unable to forget the loss and the pain he had suffered that day. He still wondered if there was something he could have done differently, or sooner, to help his father. He would always wonder. And he would never forget his father's face for as long as he lived.

Leia came gently to his side. She took his hand and led him back to the others, back into the warm circle of their love.

EAU CLAIRE DISTRICT LIBRARY.